W9-BJH-142

The
Dream
Stealer

SID FLEISCHMAN

The Dream Stealer

Pictures by
PETER SÍS

📖 Greenwillow Books
An Imprint of HarperCollinsPublishers

This book is a work of fiction. References to real people, events,
establishments, organizations, or locales are intended only to provide
a sense of authenticity, and are used to advance the fictional narrative.
All other characters, and all incidents and dialogue, are drawn from
the author's imagination and are not to be construed as real.

The Dream Stealer
Text copyright © 2009 by Sid Fleischman, Inc.
Illustrations copyright © 2009 by Peter Sís
First published in 2009 in hardcover; first paperback edition, 2011.

All rights reserved. No part of this book may be used or reproduced in any
manner whatsoever without written permission except in the case of brief
quotations embodied in critical articles and reviews. Printed in the
United States of America. For information address HarperCollins Children's Books,
a division of HarperCollins Publishers, 195 Broadway, New York, NY 10007.
www.harpercollinschildrens.com

The text of this book is set in Times New Roman.
Book design by Sylvie Le Floc'h

Library of Congress Cataloging-in-Publication Data

Fleischman, Sid, (date).
The Dream Stealer / by Sid Fleischman; illustrations by Peter Sís.
p. cm.
"Greenwillow Books."
Summary: A plucky Mexican girl tries to recover her dream from
the Dream Stealer who takes her to his castle where countless dreams
and even more adventures await.
ISBN 978-0-06-175563-7 (trade bdg.) — ISBN 978-0-06-175564-4 (lib. bdg.)
ISBN 978-0-06-178729-4 (pbk.)
[1. Dreams—Fiction. 2. Imaginary creatures—Fiction. 3. Mexico—Fiction.]
I. Sís, Peter, (date) ill. II. Title.
PZ7.F5992Dr 2009   [Fic]—dc22   2008047694

19 20 21 BRR 20 19 18 17 16 15 14 13 12

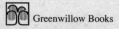 Greenwillow Books

For Pilar Armida
of Mexico City,
who introduced me to
the Dream Stealer

And for Simon

Contents

The Dream Stealer

CHAPTER 1
THE NIGHT VISITOR

Muchachos and *muchachas*, boys and girls, do you know what happened to the fearless little girl who lives in the pink stucco house behind the plaza? Fearless, but lonely. Lonely, but plucky. Do you believe in marvels?

After a long, hot day, the sun dropped behind a prickly clump of cactus without scratching itself. Then a warm night fell over the Mexican town, soft as velvet, with stars flashing like fireflies.

Bedroom windows were flung open to the evening air. Soon it would be time for Susana to go to bed. Yes, that was her name. Susana. With one *n*. Eight years old.

Unknown to her, Susana had a night visitor. Outside, a great bird with big feet was flying in as silently as an owl. It circled the pink house.

After a long journey, the strange creature came to rest on a limb of the old pepper tree in the patio of Susana's house.

A bird, did I say? Yes and no. Its wings and feathers flashed orange and red polka dots like bloodshot eyes—and green spots and purple ones, too. You'd think the night visitor had the allover measles. Now, think of teeth as sharp as broken crockery. And a full moon of a face, with cunning eyes protruding like a frog's.

An ogre? A monster? What could it be, hanging in the pepper tree like a great piñata?

I'll tell you. Be patient.

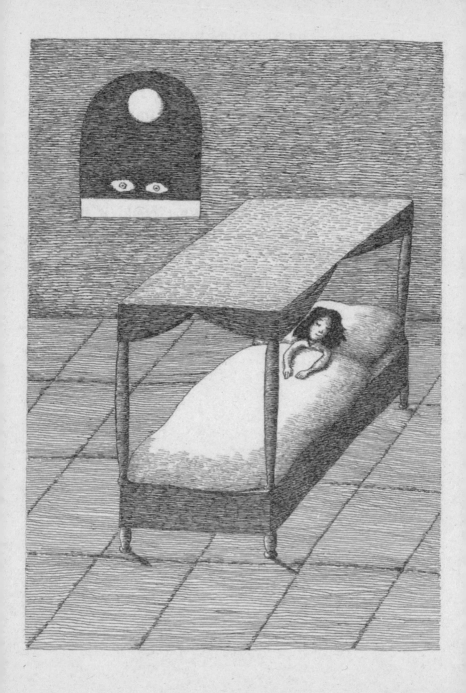

CHAPTER 2
BEDTIME FOR SUSANA

While he waited, the night visitor chewed on green chili peppers he'd picked along the way— not too mild, not too hot.

He kept a sharp eye on the windows below. Susana was hiding from her mother, first behind her father—he with the smiling black mustache. Then she ducked behind her little grandmother, who stood taking off small gold earrings.

"Time for bed, little chicken!" called out Susana's mother, Señora Cristóbal.

The girl was quickly caught, and she gave out a playful scream.

"Five more minutes, Mama!" she protested, too full of things to do to waste time sleeping.

"Not even one more second!"

The birdlike visitor grumbled impatiently. "Child, go to sleep and let's spy your dreams, yes? I don't have all night, no?" He tossed away the stem end of the green chili and started another, neither too mild nor too hot.

Susana's mother gave her daughter a good-night kiss. Before long, the lonely child with a waterfall of black hair was in bed. Across the room stood a window open to the fresh air.

Susana grew restless as she lay in the dark. She thought of her best friend, Consuelo Louisa. They had had a noisy argument playing soccer and were no longer best friends. The two had even stopped talking to each other. And now Consuelo Louisa had moved away, to far-off Guadalajara, in the north.

Susana wanted to cry. "And I don't like you for moving away!" she mumbled to herself. She knew it was not Consuelo Louisa's fault, but she blamed her anyway. Consuelo Louisa had left their village without even saying good-bye, adios, Susana, I'll write you a letter. Now, secret tears crept into the bedtime girl's eyes. She wouldn't allow anyone to see how lonely she was. Abandoned as a fallen leaf. She would never see her very best friend ever again.

She turned over in bed, but it did no good. She counted sheep. She counted burros. She counted tortillas, burned to a crisp.

Laughing Consuelo Louisa would make new friends in the big city. She would forget Susana, left behind in the country. Perhaps she had forgotten already! It was too painful to imagine.

High in the tree, the stranger used a wing to fan his chili breath, now warm as a furnace. When was that wretched child going to fall asleep and begin dreaming?

For the stranger was a shameless thief. Not a

bandit after silver earrings and gold necklaces. He cared nothing for diamonds and rubies. He was a burglar of other people's dreams.

I promised to tell you. He was the famous and prowling Dream Stealer.

CHAPTER 3
Susana Dreaming

Had Susana peered out her bedroom window, she might have noticed the fine lasso the Dream Stealer carried over one shoulder—yes, he had arms as long as yours or mine.

The lasso was braided of the finest spiders' silk. It was strong. Strong as steel.

He'd fling it out and lasso bad dreams—

screaming nightmares! Horrors! Botherations! He'd stuff them into a black bag around his waist and streak off into the night as silently as he'd arrived.

But he'd grown frightened of other people's beasts and bad dreams. The sight of misshapen monsters and snarling phantoms made his feathers tremble and shake.

Night after night, the Dream Stealer had been catching and making off with happy dreams. Who was to tell him he couldn't?

Susana fell asleep at last. Before long, she dreamed of balancing a spelling book on her head as she walked to school. The Dream Stealer gave a snort of boredom.

Then, in her sleep, Susana began to giggle.

She was dreaming of Consuelo Louisa as if they were still best friends and still lived across the plaza from each other. The girls were playing tag around the empty bandstand.

Presto! The bandstand turned into a merry-go-round with live horses. The two playmates jumped on and galloped off, giggling and laughing together.

The Dream Stealer tossed away his half-eaten green chili pepper. This was more like it! Slipping the lariat from his shoulder, he closed one eye and took aim at the open window with the other.

Now the girls were racing along a shallow riverbed, splashing as they went. The Dream Stealer flung his lariat. In that instant, Consuelo

Louisa's horse tripped. Susana gasped as she saw her friend tossed into midair and about to fall on the river rocks.

The lariat flew through the window. Quick as a lizard's tongue, it caught the dream. In the treetop, the thief hauled in the happy scene, horses and all. He stuffed the dream into the black sack around his waist.

Susana awoke in bed with a gasp. What had happened? Like a windblown match, the dream had gone dark. Consuelo Louisa was left in the air, about to fall. She'd be hurt on the rocks!

Susana sat up, angry. Where was the rest of her dream? It was almost a month since she and Consuelo Louisa had played together. And there they had been, screaming with fun. Susana had been thrilled. But now her best friend might be broken like a vase against the rocks. Were her cuts bleeding into the river? She might be calling Susana to help her. She might even be dying.

A new worry caught hold of Susana's thoughts. Did dreams tell the future? Could they? Her grandmother had no doubts when she studied tea leaves. And what about the man in the sunglasses who came to the plaza on Sundays to read fortunes with a greasy pack of cards?

Susana laid her head back on the pillow and shut her eyes on the confusion whirling inside her head. She tried to force herself to go back to sleep. She needed to finish her dream. She not only yearned for the presence of her closest friend, Susana had to know what the dream had been trying to tell her. If Consuelo Louisa's life would end on the river rocks, would her days end soon, too, in far-off Guadalajara? What a bad, perfectly terrible dream!

The Dream Stealer remained in the pepper tree only to free his spiders' silk lasso, caught on the foliage. Losing nothing but a feather, he silently flew off to plunder another dream or two in town. But first he paused in an avocado tree and ate one or two fruits, leaving a garbage of green peelings behind.

CHAPTER 4

Clues Under
the Pepper Tree

When Susana returned from school the next
day, her mind was bubbling with a plan. The
night before, she had commanded her dream
to return, but it had refused to be ordered
about. Other scenes filled her sleep—a show-
off tarantula skipping rope, but no Consuelo
Louisa. The shy new boy at school kicking a

soccer ball over the fence — what was his name? But no Consuelo Louisa.

After greeting her mother and grandmother, Susana headed for the patio. In the fishnet hammock, stretched out in the shade of the pepper tree, she wrapped herself tight as a cocoon. When she discovered the stem end of a green chili pressed against her cheek, she impatiently brushed it away.

Other chili stems lay scattered on the ground, but she barely noticed them.

Once more Susana commanded herself to dream — that was her plan. How could she expect to dream if she weren't asleep? She held her eyes tightly closed. She tried to shut out the sounds of cars blowing their noisy horns in the plaza.

Sleep eluded her.

It seemed an hour, but it wasn't, when she blew air from her cheeks like wind escaping a balloon. How could she take a siesta when she was so wide awake? Dreaming was impossible.

She slipped out of the hammock. She'd wait for night to try again. Consuelo Louisa would be quite safe left in midair a few hours longer. "I hope you're not too frightened up there," she said aloud, as if her friend could hear her. "Maybe at the end of the dream I caught you and you weren't hurt at all."

Touching the ground, Susana's foot disturbed a feather. She paused for a second look. Some migrating bird must have dropped it, she thought. How big it was! Too big for a crow or even a hawk. And what strange colors—purple with orange spots and orange with purple spots, all looking at her like wide-awake eyes.

She plucked up the feather and, at dinner, asked her grandmother about it.

"That?" replied the straight-backed old woman with a flash of her brand-new teeth. "I haven't seen such a feather since I was a child."

"You know what bird dropped it?"

"Not a bird. More like a hog with wings!"

"*Abuelita!* Grandmother! Don't tease me! A hog flying about our patio?"

"The impudent hombre! Did he leave garbage after him?"

"Like chili stems?" asked Susana.

"Like anything! *Ay-ya-ya-ya-ya!* Susanita, that

feather belonged to a grouchy Dream Stealer."

"A what? A Dream Stealer?"

"What else? The creature flies at night and snatches away your monsters and ogres and nightmares."

"Why?"

"The bad dreams. So you can sleep."

"Last night, I think he stole my dream!" Susana said with a flash of anger. "But there were no monsters or ogres in it."

Susana's grandmother shrugged. "Oh, sometimes the Dream Stealer is so grouchy, he forgets what he's doing. He's not to be trusted."

"Why would he be grouchy, doing everyone the favor of stealing their nightmares?" asked Susana.

"Child, if all your companions were ogres and monsters, you'd be grouchy, too."

"But I wasn't finished with my dream!" Susana protested. "I want it back!"

"Don't talk nonsense," said her father, Señor Cristóbal, using a finger to brush back his mustache as if he were grooming a horse.

Said Susana, "In my dream, Consuelo Louisa was thrown off her saddle! What if she's hurt?"

"Dreams are not to be believed," said her father. "They are loco fumes from inside the head, eh? Craziness."

"Loco? Craziness?" protested Susana's grandmother. "Didn't I dream three years ago that I would find a twenty-peso bill?"

"And last week you found a ten-centavo

coin," said Susana's father, bursting into a laugh. "You should get your money back on that dream. Old woman, don't forget the old saying: 'We don't need to study to become a fool!'"

"My tea leaves speak the truth!" the grandmother replied.

"Sí," replied Señor Cristóbal. "They foretell that your cup of tea will keep you wide awake all night!"

Susana looked up at her mother to settle matters. Did *she* think the dream was a warning that Consuelo Louisa was truly in danger?

But all her mother said was, "Eat before the soup gets cold."

CHAPTER 5
The Trap

Later that night, Susana slipped out of bed to keep watch from the window. She hoped the Dream Stealer would return. She'd climb through the window and demand that he give back her stolen dream. And please, don't come back!

She could hear the big old family clock in the hall striking off the seconds. Before long, her eyelids began to feel weighted. She propped them open with her fingers. Soon her fingers tired. She was hardly aware of falling asleep on her arms folded across the windowsill.

She awoke the next morning in bed. Her mother must have carried her there in her sleep.

Leaving for school, she noticed fresh chili stems under the pepper tree. She had missed the Dream Stealer! She felt a flash of fury to have missed him.

A new idea gripped her when she recalled the bag of fiery red chilis her father had brought home from Uncle Pablo's garden. Hot? Hot as blowtorches! You had to have a fireproof mouth to eat them raw. For cooking, her mother wouldn't scrape out the seeds without first putting on rubber gloves.

Well before dinner, Susana slipped on the kitchen gloves and picked out eight of the scalding hot chilis. She painted them with green food coloring and smiled at her artistry. "Nibble on these!" she said aloud, as if the Dream Stealer were asleep on the kitchen chair. "I'll catch you like a hungry bobcat!"

Before going to bed, she set out the bowl of painted chilis under the pepper tree. One bite and he'd howl loud enough to wake snakes. And wake her, too!

Of course he'd beg for water. She put a pitcher of cool water on the windowsill and confidently fell asleep. She dreamed of painted green chilis dancing around a sombrero.

CHAPTER 6
A Secret Destination

Like an alarm clock going off, a burst of yowling and coughing shook the leaves of the pepper tree. In bed, Susana kicked away her covers and rushed to the window.

"Bandit! Is that you, Dream Stealer?" she shouted.

"Water! Oh, water!" came the reply, and now

Susana could see the fabled night creature up in the tree. His face glowed as red as a lantern. All his feathers tried to fan him at once.

"It's about time you showed up!" she called out. "Here's the water pitcher waiting for you."

The Dream Stealer tumbled out of the tree and half flew, half lurched to the window.

"Was it you who loaded those chilis with swamp fire?"

"I did. And it was you who stole my dream!"

"You had no further use for it," he croaked, and took a long drink to put out the fire in his throat.

"Yes, I do! Give it back!" Susana shouted.

"Ba!"

"It's mine!"

"Bosh!"

"I didn't finish dreaming!"

"So what?" he replied grouchily.

"I want it back!"

"Ba! Bosh!"

Susana swept the hair out of her eyes. "How can you be so mean?"

"It's a talent I have."

"And how dare you spy on people's dreams! Is that polite?"

"Was it polite to turn my throat into a fire pit?"

Almost bursting into tears, Susana snapped, "I want my dream back, Señor Dream Stealer!"

"Do you think I carry yesterday's dreams around in my pockets like old crusts of bread? See, I have no pockets."

"You have a black bag."

"Empty. Want to see for yourself, nosy child?"

"Where did you hide my dream?"

"Does a magician tell where he hides his rabbits?"

"You're not a magician. You're a bandit!"

"A bit of both, little señorita," the creature said, grinning. "What is a dream but a passing trifle? A sneeze between the ears, no? So why not go back to sleep and dream yourself fresh sneezes by the wagonload, yes?"

Said Susana fiercely, astonished by her expanding courage, "I don't want a new dream! I want my old one! Thief! Burglar!"

"Give back a dream. Huh! More water, if you please."

"I don't please. No dream, no water, señor!"

Susana's eyebrows stiffened, low and defiant. She had lost Consuelo Louisa over a silly argument, and a second time to the Dream Stealer. Wild horses couldn't stop Susana now.

"Well?"

"Troublesome child! I make no limp-hearted returns! You want me to become a laughingstock? Give back? What horrible nonsense! I'd be ruined."

"You steal from children! That will ruin your reputation!"

"Not a bit! Tots are happy that I steal their nightmares."

Susana shook her head. "I wasn't having a nightmare! We were having fun, Consuelo Louisa and I."

The Dream Stealer had gotten his head stuck in

the pitcher seeking a last drop. His voice sounded hollow, as if from a well. "Say I return everyone's dreams like dropped handkerchiefs! Eh? Wide-awake sleepers will grit their teeth at me for giving back their bad dreams." He pulled his head free. "I'd be snickered and hee-hawed as a failure at the fine old trade of dream stealing. A dream giver-backer! A giver-backer of dreams! What an insult to my proud ancestors! Never, child!"

Susana wasn't swayed. "You'll be hee-hawed and guffawed when everyone finds out you steal happy dreams! Full of laughing! Everyone knows you're only supposed to steal scary nightmares."

"Shhh!"

"When Consuelo Louisa fell off her horse, it

happened in the blink of an eye! You didn't see my dream turn bad, did you?"

The night visitor fanned his mouth with a tail feather. "Mistakes happen."

"It was no mistake! You carried off a happy dream, and I'm going to tell everyone!"

The color drained out of the Dream Stealer's face. "You wouldn't!"

"I would!"

"Pesky child. All right. I'm sorry. Now skip the noise."

"Sorry isn't good enough!" Susana replied. "Hand over what's mine."

The Dream Stealer's eyes sagged like old button-holes. Finally he said, "If I give back your dream, promise you won't breathe a word?"

"I don't trust bandits. First hand over my dream, horses and all!"

"It'll take a little time. I can do no better."

She believed him, and relented. She picked up the empty water pitcher.

"Thank you, little lady. Your little dream is stored with hundreds of others. Thousands."

"Where? I won't tell your hiding place."

"In my castle."

It hadn't occurred to Susana that the Dream Stealer lived anywhere special. "You have a castle?" she murmured, trying not to sound impressed. "There's no castle around here, Señor Dream Stealer."

"Fetch the water, please."

"I've never been in a castle," Susana said

with grudging interest. She refilled the pitcher and brought it back.

After a long drink, the night visitor's frog eyes gave a weary blink. "Alas, child. The dreams are stored far away."

Susana's heart gave a joyful leap. "How far is far? I'll go!"

"Foolish child. Have you ever flown in the air?"

"Of course not."

"Are you afraid of heights?"

"Certainly not."

"Once you climb through your window, it'll be too late to change your mind."

Susana didn't hesitate. "Just make sure I get back before my parents wake up in the morning and miss me. I'm Susana. What's your name?"

"You may call me Zumpango, since that is not my name."

"What is it, then?"

"It's whatever I say it is, bumptious child. Muster up your courage and we'll be off! Hurry!"

CHAPTER 7
THE NIGHT TRAVELERS

Quickly Susana got into her pink robe and double-knotted the sash. She crawled through the window, allowing herself a victorious smile. Change her mind? Never!

The Dream Stealer—Zumpango—drained the pitcher of its last drop of water. "Just grab my ankles and hang on," he commanded. Shaking out his wings as if opening an umbrella, he took a little run and was quickly airborne.

"Hey!" Susana cried out. "Wait for me!"

The creature made a swing around the pepper tree to build up a modest speed. He reappeared, hovering just above the ground. Susana caught his ankles and was yanked off her feet.

"Don't let go!" he said.

"I won't!"

When Susana looked down, they were rising up over the pepper tree and the sleeping house below. How could she fail to let a small gasp escape? Her parents would yell themselves hoarse if they saw her up in the sky. If she was feeling afraid, she refused to admit it. She'd be brave, even if she had to pretend.

Soon they crossed over the quiet town, its window shades drawn like eyelids asleep for the night.

"Where are we going?" Susana shouted.

"I told you," replied the Dream Stealer. "It's my secret! Do I want nosy strangers banging at my castle doors and stealing souvenirs? Close your peepers."

"My what?"

"Your lamps. Your eyes."

"But I want to see the sights."

"Shut them tight! No spying! If you pop them open, I'll drop you like a stone."

"You wouldn't." But Susana took an even firmer grip on his ankles. What a bully he was, she thought! She clamped her eyes shut.

"Tight as walnuts?" he asked.

"See for yourself."

He turned his head around for a look. "And no peeking."

Off they flew, through the darkness. When Susana smelled honeysuckles in the air, she knew they had turned north where the plants grew wild on the bank of the river. And when she caught the scent of greasewood and mesquite, she knew they were crossing the desert.

She heard the wind whistle between her toes. Her long hair shot out behind her as straight as arrows. How swiftly they were flying!

The air was getting colder. Soon she smelled pine needles. Mountains!

"Your feet are dragging," the Dream Stealer

called out. "Straighten them like sticks!"

"They're freezing. How much farther?"

"You'll see."

"How fast are you flying?" Susana asked.

"Have you ever been shot out of a cannon?"

"Of course not."

"That's how fast, brave child."

They fell silent. She began to wonder if the flight were fueled with magic. Hardly three minutes could have passed when the Dream Stealer said, "See that sharp mountain cliff?"

"How can I see with my eyes shut?"

"Open them. And, little señorita Susana, don't stub your toe when we land."

CHAPTER 8

Guests in the Dungeon

Susana saw the mountain cliff rushing toward her. Behind it there rose an unkempt castle. It poked the sky with its towers, each holding aloft moldy red roofs as pointed as dunce caps. Trees crowded in on the palace like brooding guards on duty.

His wings beating furiously, Zumpango came

in to land. He lit, rather clumsily, on the carpet of lumpy cobblestones laid out before the entry doors. Susana did stub her toe, but she refused to let out a cry. She wouldn't allow the Dream Stealer to scowl at her for being a nuisance.

He banged on the door, and in due time a small panel slid open. A pair of gray eyes peered out.

"Who is it, sir?"

Said the Dream Stealer, "Who are you expecting? Little Red Riding Hood? It's me!"

"I believe you mean 'whom,' sir."

"*Who! Whom!* Idiot! Open up!"

"Of course, milord. I wasn't expecting you back so early."

"A butler should expect anything!"

Susana raised an eyebrow to Zumpango.

"Why do you need a butler to open doors? You said you don't have visitors."

"Time to give my castle a smack of nobility. I found this snooty butler in someone's dream and put him to his trade."

Susana's head began to spin. The butler was a dream? The door swung open, and she found herself staring at the long-faced servant in his black coat and black shoes and stiff white collar. He hardly looked airy and the stuff of dreams. Was she to believe her eyes? He looked quite as solid as a tree.

"Come along, child," said Zumpango. "I don't have all night to find this foolish friend of yours."

Susana followed her host into a vast candlelit hall. The butler backed away and slowly vanished into the shadows. Susana had a sense that the Dream Stealer not only had no visitors, he had no friends.

To her right, a door stood ajar, with what appeared to be prison bars behind it blocking the way. She glimpsed several look-alikes wearing red suits and beards as sharp as church steeples. Stubby horns grew from their heads. They carried pitchforks like walking sticks. Devils?

"What else? People *will* dream of Beelzebubs and imps and Lucifers and Old Splitfoots," declared the Dream Stealer with an impatient *harrumph*. "Must keep matches away from those nightmare fellows. They are so careless with fire."

Across the way, Susana read a huge sign over

an iron door: DUNGEON FOR GUESTS ONLY! KEEP OUT! She could hear yells and yowls and growls behind the door.

"Do you keep dreams locked in the dungeon?"

He nodded wearily. "Not mere dreams. Nightmares! Horrors! Bad dreams that'll turn your blood cold!"

"It says guests."

"Your friend is not there."

Could she trust him? "I'd like to see for myself," said Susana.

"Pesky child!" He picked her up so that her eye could reach a peephole in the door. "Don't tell me what ogres and monsters you see! One sight will curdle milk! Such horrors. I shake when I think of them!"

"They're only dreams, Señor Zumpango. You know they're not real."

"Do I? Then why am I trembling already?"

Susana took a breath. What about the butler in his high stiff collar, she wondered? How could he look so real?

She put her eye to the peephole. She saw a vast stone cellar. It was crowded with frightful demons! Scary dreams! No doubt Zumpango had collected them before his courage gave out.

Susana caught sight of vampires flying about like squealing bats. She saw hairy monsters snarling at one another. She glimpsed snakes as big around as telephone poles. And ogres galore, with hair as wild as weeds. Rats, too. The size of rowboats!

She gave an inward shiver.

Across the room sat a two-headed giant. Both his noses were as shapeless as overripe tomatoes. One head wore a black eye patch. Manacled to a stone wall, the giant appeared to be talking in his sleep. From both sets of lips came the booming of a duet that sounded somewhat familiar to Susana.

> *"Fe fo fi fum! We smells the blood of Lord*
>   *Zumpango!*
> *Be he far or be he near, we'll grind his bones*
> *And dance the tango!"*

Susana pulled away, glad she had been spared visits from such scary night visitors. To her host, she said, "I don't think that two-headed giant likes you."

The Dream Stealer dismissed the matter with a shrug. "They're chained like bulls. Worry not. Follow me."

Up a narrow flight of stairs, they passed a wide-open door. The room behind was heaped with great piles of small white teeth. Hills of them. Mountains of them. Said the Dream Stealer, "See that man in bed with his head wrapped in hot towels and his nose red as ketchup? That's the Tooth Fairy, down with a bad cold."

"He lives here?" exclaimed Susana.

"He's got to live somewhere."

"But I don't believe in tooth fairies."

The creature in the four-poster bed gave a loud sneeze and reached for a fresh handkerchief.

"No? Who do you think just sneezed and blew his nose? And where did those snowbanks of baby teeth come from?"

"You're trying to confuse me," Susana protested. "I'm too old to believe in tooth fairies! That's for little kids!"

"Suit yourself."

They continued on to the floor above.

"We're here, child."

"Where?"

He threw open the door to a white bedroom, lifeless, except for a confusion of fireflies flitting about in the dimness. A bed stood enclosed in dusty mosquito netting. Moonlight shot through the deep-set castle windows.

"This is where I store the dreams that you

children make in such thoughtless abundance."

Susana entered the room and brushed aside a firefly landing on her forehead. "I don't see any storage boxes."

"Do you think those are fireflies?"

"Aren't they?"

"Not real ones."

Susana brushed off another bug. She caught it and looked more closely. It wasn't real. "You've turned make-believe dreams into make-believe fireflies?"

"Think of the space they save! Now, let's find your dream flying around with its light blinking. Watch."

CHAPTER 9

𝒜 𝖥𝗂𝗋𝖾𝖿𝗅𝗒 𝗂𝗇 𝗍𝗁𝖾 𝖧𝖺𝗇𝖽

The Dream Stealer closed the door behind them and caught a firefly in his bare hand. "Observe," he said, and slowly opened his fingers.

Susana watched the firefly unfold like a flower, revealing a dream flashing on the palm of his hand. Amazed, she saw a boy climbing a coconut tree.

"Simple magic, no?" said the Dream Stealer. "You can do it. Catch one."

Susana's heart was sinking fast. "But there are so many! It could take weeks to find Consuelo Louisa!"

"Perhaps not, child. See how the lights are growing dim on the older dreams? Catch the fresh ones."

Susana reached out a hand and caught a bright firefly. It showed a crocodile eating spaghetti. The Dream Stealer told her to discard it behind the bed's mosquito curtains to avoid catching it again.

And so an hour passed. Accustomed to being sound asleep past midnight, Susana was finding it difficult to keep her eyes open. She sat on an oak bench and continued searching the fireflies.

Unaware, she nodded off. A dream of her own filled her head. Tonight she was balancing a branch of red-hot chili peppers on her chin. And then the vision went suddenly dark.

The Dream Stealer gave a small grin. "I woke you, no? I stole your new dream before it could grow horses and Consuelos to confuse us."

He handed her the freshly hatched firefly, as bright as the flare of a match. Instead of turning it loose, she buried it in the pocket of her robe and put her embroidered handkerchief over it. When she got home, the magic firefly would prove to her family that her adventure had really happened.

She rubbed her eyes to get the sleep out and

resumed the search. She found dogs and bobcats and two boys fighting in the mud. She was quick to discard the useless fireflies behind the mosquito netting.

Suddenly the Dream Stealer's palm appeared in front of her face. "This is you, yes?"

There, on his open hand, Susana saw children at a birthday party. She shrugged. "We were riding merry-go-round horses in my dream— where are the horses?"

"So, my little friend?"

So we keep looking. And I'm not your little friend, Susana thought. But when she looked more closely at the dream in Zumpango's hand, she gave a full gasp. She saw *herself*, Susana Cristóbal, at the birthday party.

What was she doing there? This was not her dream. It must be Consuelo Louisa's!

Yes! That was her! That was Susana's faraway friend, Consuelo, in the yellow taffeta party dress!

And look! She was blowing out the candles. It was Consuelo Louisa's birthday party! And who was that seated beside her?

Me, Susana saw. It's me!

Susana almost shouted, "Consuelo Louisa's birthday was just two days ago! Do you see? She didn't get hurt in the river. There she is, without so much as a scratch!"

"Splendid. Still, that is not the dream we came so far to find."

He was interrupted by a great noise along

the hall. The door flew open, and there stood the butler, his clothes ripped to rags.

"If I may interrupt, sir?" he said.

"You may not!"

"But sir."

"Go tend the front doors," insisted Zumpango.

"That's the very point, milord."

"What are you talking about?"

"The doors have been ripped off their hinges, sir."

"No one could do that but that stupid two-headed giant, Thunderdel."

"Exactly, sir."

"But he's in irons."

"No longer."

"Thunderdel has escaped his chains?"

"Escaped the dungeon, too."

"Horrors!"

"Indeed. And he has freed the other monsters and ogres. You might consider hiding, sir, as Thunderdel seems rather out of sorts. In fact, here he comes."

CHAPTER 10
THE CHASE

Galumphing along the hall, Thunderdel tossed the butler aside with a swipe of his arm. The two-headed giant spotted the Dream Stealer and gave out a windy duet.

"Fi fi fum fo!
Run for thy life, Zumpango!

We'll crack thy head with a two-by-four

And rattle thy ears on the kitchen floor

And grind thy bones as fine as pepper

And sneeze thee out the door!"

Beside her, Susana saw the Dream Stealer go pale and begin to tremble. His feet spun, and he quickly was half flying along the hall and around a corner.

She ran, too, forgetting to shut the door. Fireflies flowed into the hall and scattered into passageways and down stairways. Susana almost paused to gasp, but there wasn't time. Her old dream would be lost! It might even find the front doors broken open and fly away into the night.

She had caught a flash of Zumpango vanishing up the tower stairway. Heart in her throat, she waved her arms. She was a fast runner at school and would lead the ogre on a wild chase. If he caught the Dream Stealer and ground him up, how would Susana ever get home?

"Excuse me, sir!" she called out. "Giant! Thunder-whatever-your-name-is! Here I am! Grind me up and spit out my ears, if you like!"

Boldly, she kept her arms waving and then ran along the hall. Thunderdel refused to follow. Instead he went crashing on his big feet toward the tower, toward the Dream Stealer.

"Brother!" said one of the giant's heads, with

two blinking eyes. "Why would 'e go up there to be trapped in a tower, I ask ya? Down the hall, says I!"

"Up the tower, says I," replied the eye-patched other head. "I smells the blood of an Englishman!"

"That was long ago, brother! And I smells the blood of that feathered varmint Zumpango! This way!"

"The tower, or I'll hang your guts on a fence to dry!"

"They'll be your guts, too, brother!"

"I'll be pleased to settle your argument," Susana called out, bravely, but trembling inside. "Just follow me! I'll show you the way to the feathered varmint!"

"And who be you?" called out Eye Patch.

"Susana, and so glad to oblige a genuine two-headed giant. This way, señores! This way, gentlemen!"

"She's playing a trick!" said Eye Patch.

"Follow me and find out!" taunted Susana.

"Go away!"

"Flee, little flea!"

Susana now jumped up and down to tease them. "You afraid of a little squeak of a girl like me?"

"We catch you like a mouse!" Two Eyes snarled.

"And use your toes for toothpicks!" promised Eye Patch.

"A little later, little lady!"

"We got bigger game to chase!"

Susana was astonished at her own fearlessness. "You can't fool a mouse like me!

Elephants are afraid of mice. So are you!"

Now the two heads roared in unison, and the black eye patch fluttered as if it were the lid of a boiling pot. The creature came thundering toward her, snorting like a pair of bulls.

And so began a wild chase through the castle. The lumbering giant swept away chandeliers as if they were cobwebs. He banged into the kitchens, sending pots and pans flying. And still he could not catch Susana. With his big, oafish feet, he was no match for Susana's young legs.

She jumped stairs. She leaped over barrels.

Once she swung away on a bell rope.

Everywhere she ran, she saw fireflies. They swarmed in the halls and chambers. They discovered a broken window and some escaped into the night. Gone forever.

Shouted the giant in a thundering duet,

"Fi fo fi fums! We'll gobble thee up for
   breakfast
And leave nothing but thy crumbs!"

The monster was awfully close, Susana realized. With a flash of relief, she saw coming between them a vampire and a horrible boa constrictor that had followed Thunderdel to freedom. The irritable giant tossed the vampire into a heap and tied the snake into a knot the reptile wouldn't be able to undo for days.

Backed against a stone wall, Susana was

alarmed to recognize the tower entry near where she now stood. The race around the castle had led her back to the tower stairway where Zumpango had run to hide.

With the giant's arms reaching out like claws to grab her, Susana saw no choice. She slipped through the stone entryway and took the stairs two at a time. Above her head, she saw the staircase winding round and round to the top of the tower. She hoped that the Dream Stealer had long ago made his escape.

But, and alas, I must tell you that he had not.

CHAPTER 11
GULP!

Like the tail of a comet, the giant followed Susana up the winding stairs to the tower. She could hear one head chuckling and the other *fe-fi-fo-fum*ming at her heels. The tower and the stairs became narrower as they rose, and Susana felt the walls growing snug around her. Still, she had room to spare. Within moments she heard huffing and puffing below. The giant was filling the tight stairwell and was forced to squeeze himself like toothpaste in a tube. He was slowed down.

Thunder-something-or-other? What was his name? *Thunderdel?* She remembered now! He was the two-headed ogre in her storybook about Jack the Giant Killer. Some careless child must have dreamed about the cruel giant from the olden tale. And now there he was, at her heels, snapping his jaws like a crocodile.

Her heart was thumping and banging. When her head popped into the tower room, she saw that the Dream Stealer had tried to escape feet first through the narrow stone window. He was stuck there like a fat cork in a bottle.

"The giant is coming!" Susana cried out. "Can't you wriggle through?"

"Give a push, dear friend!"

She put her weight against his shoulder but only succeeded in plugging him even tighter in the window.

"Save yourself, child! Run for your life!"

Susana thought that was a generous notion, except that she was caught between the Dream Stealer, stuck in the window, and the giant below, wriggling like a two-headed snake to free himself from the tight walls and pop through into the tower room.

"He's just a bad dream come to life," Susana heard herself say, amazed to be able to open her mouth and find her voice lurking there. "Let me think what to do."

"Don't be all a-flutter and a-tremble," the Dream Stealer burst out, clearly a-flutter and a-tremble himself. "Be brave!"

"Hmm. What if he's made of nothing but cobwebs and thistledown and thin air? And not very bright, is he?"

"Bright enough to grind bones!"

Susana crossed back to the stairs and looked down at the giant struggling upward and gaining another step. "Famous giant!" she called out. "What do you think? The Dream Stealer was foolish enough to get stuck in the tower window? Isn't that funny? Ha-ha! You might as well climb back down."

"We're hungry, lass! You'll make a tidy breakfast, you will," Eye Patch thundered.

"Aye, with a swallow a' rum!" Two Eyes added. "Fe fi fo fum!"

"I wouldn't like that," answered Susana, whose hand was already searching the pocket of her robe. Was the firefly she'd tucked in still there?

She found it. Quickly she let her short dream of hours before unfold in her hand. There she saw herself, with the tiny branch of hot red chilis balanced on her chin like candle flames.

Carefully she lifted off the branch, and the red-hot chilis expanded to their living size.

Grimly, she looked down at Thunderdel, squirming inches below her. Only Eye Patch's mouth hung wide open, slavering like a dog's. One mouth would be enough.

Susana let go of the branch. Down the open throat it fell. The chilis must have tickled. Eye Patch coughed and ground his teeth, tearing open several red-hot chilis. He might as well have lit matches to kindling. He gave a great howl and a choking gulp. His mouth and throat were all but in flames.

The giant now erupted heat like a volcano. The fumes alone almost blew Susana to the roof.

"What is it, brother?" asked baffled Two Eyes, seeing his adjoining head glow red as neon.

"*WATER! WATER!*" croaked out Eye Patch.

Hardly a second passed before the giant vanished. Dragging his brother with him, Eye Patch unplugged his shoulders from the stairway. The giant bumped and boomed like a boulder to the hall below, bellowing for water.

In huge relief, Susana paused only for a sigh and turned to the Dream Stealer. "You can come out now," she said.

"Fearless child! Pull me free!"

She caught him under the wings, braced a foot against the wall, and pulled hard. He came unplugged, knocking her down.

She brushed herself off and stuck her head out the window to look down. Far down. "You could have been killed falling out of this window."

The Dream Stealer was shaking his colored feathers back in place. "I have the skills of a bird, remember?"

"You promised to fly me home. Remember?"

"In due time." Zumpango began inflating

his chest as if filling it with new courage. "How fearless you were. Reminds me of me in my youth."

"Look at the giant running down there."

The Dream Stealer paused to glance down. "What's that confounded giant doing below, at the well? Jumping in?"

"He seems to be taken with a great thirst," she said.

CHAPTER 12
ALL'S WELL

Susana said, "Señor Zumpango, will it soon be dawn? You must keep your word and fly me home."

But the Dream Stealer was already leaping down the stairs, round and round. Susana refused to let him out of her sight and raced after him.

In the great hall below, he picked up a coach whip. He cracked it in the air at a snarling pirate.

And again, like a lion tamer, at a rat the size of a rowboat. "Back! Back!" he shouted, bursting with courage. "Does it insult your ugliness to live in a grand castle? How long do you think you'd last in the wild forest outside? Coarse dreams! I again see you for what you are. Wispy phantoms! Flimsy savages! Into the grand ballroom, ungrateful guests! Where's my butler?"

"Here, sir."

"I'll teach the villains to be civilized. To behave like gentlemen—like me! Until then, lock them in, no?"

"Yes, sir."

Susana gazed in bewilderment at the Dream Stealer. Was he no longer terrified of the monsters? What had come over him?

"You, fearless child. Reminded me of Zumpango in his callow youth. Brave as a lion, was I! A tiger! A snapping turtle! A cross-eyed zebra! A brass monkey! A—"

"I get the idea, sir."

Chest puffed up with restored boldness, he strode through the broken entry doors and around to the stables. Susana thought she glimpsed unicorns in the stalls, but horses, too.

Nearby in the weed-grown courtyard stood the castle well. Thunderdel's faded green boots were now flailing the air. Had he jumped into the well and couldn't get out? He had and he couldn't.

Off his shoulder, the Dream Stealer shook the coil of spiders' silk lasso. Strong as steel, that lasso, you'll recall. He caught the giant's ankles and hitched up a pair of horses. He plucked the half-drowned Thunderdel out of the well, the giant squealing like a rusty hinge. Soon the monster's wrists were tied together behind his back.

"Now, you big oaf," thundered the Dream Stealer, "I'm tired of allowing you to frighten me out of my feathers and chasing me in my own castle! What are you made of but cobwebs and thistledown and thin air! I don't think you could grind my bones, alive or dead, not with both your confounded mouths full of ugly teeth! Noisy braggarts! Nonsense fellows! I'm going to teach you to behave yourselves! Aye, if you want to live unchained in my castle you'll have to dress for dinner. And stop picking your teeth with tent poles. And take a bath at least twice a year. Otherwise, it's back in the dungeon for the two of you!"

The horses dragged the two-headed giant bumping and bouncing back into the castle. Susana gazed at the Dream Stealer with new admiration.

"That was very brave," she said.

Zumpango lifted his chin half an inch into the air. "Yes, wasn't it? Now we must find your dream."

"No, sir. I fear it's flown into the night. And it won't be necessary. I got invited to Consuelo Louisa's birthday, and she was alive without a single bruise from falling off her horse! And she had me sit beside her, like best friends. I must send her a birthday present, don't you think?"

"So it's finished, is it, little Señorita Susana?

I kept my word. Now you must keep yours, and not tell a soul what a soft heart I have."

"But you do have a soft heart!"

"Shhh. It would create a scandal."

She nodded. "I'll keep your silly secret. But if you ever change your mind—"

"Grab my ankles," said the Dream Stealer.

CHAPTER 13

GOOD-BYE, ZUMPANGO

The flight home seemed to last no more than a few minutes plus a few minutes and add a few minutes more. Holding on to the Dream Stealer's legs, Susana remembered to keep her eyes tightly shut.

She would always wonder where his castle lay hidden in the faraway mountains. Somewhere beyond the desert, she knew. Somewhere beyond the smell of honeysuckles.

"You may snap open your eyes," called out the Dream Stealer.

They were circling the pepper tree in the patio of her home.

"Don't stub your toe, little Miss Susana."

They landed gently, and she felt the comfort of her own yard under her feet. "Thank you, señor. Gracias, sir."

"For nothing, no?"

"For kindness, yes. I think you are nice even when you are not nice."

"Me?"

"Do you have a best friend?"

"Bosh!"

"If you promise to stop stealing happy dreams, I will be your friend."

Zumpango blushed a little and shook his feathers in place. "Agreed! Your good dreams will be safe from me. But nightmares, watch out! Zumpango is fearless!"

"Good-bye, good-bye."

"Adios, adios!"

And off he flew into the night air until Susana could see him no longer. For a few hours, she realized, he had become her best friend, next to Consuelo Louisa. She felt a great burden lifted to know that way up in Guadalajara, Consuelo Louisa hadn't forgotten her. They were still best friends, maybe not for always, but for a while longer.

How surprising it was to have made a friend of the Dream Stealer. She began to wonder about that new boy at school, forever kicking the soccer ball, who seemed to like her. He looked shy and lonely. Maybe she'd talk to him.

She crawled back through her open bedroom window. She got back between the covers and thought of the perils of her night's adventure. *"Ay-ya-ya-ya-ya!"* she muttered, imitating her grandmother. Before long, exhausted, Susana fell sound asleep.

She dreamed the morning sun was streaming in and her mother was trying to awaken her. "Eyes open, little bedbug! The telephone. It's for you!"

For an instant, the dream went dark. Was

her friend the Dream Stealer at it again? But no! She came awake and saw her mother staring down at her. This wasn't a dream. It was real. "Wake up, child. The telephone."

Susana pressed the phone to her sleepy ear. "Hola," she said. "Hello."

A voice in her ear answered back, "Hola. This is Consuelo Louisa, and oh, how I have missed you."

Susana sat up as if lifted by lightning. "I have missed you, too!"

"Now that I'm nine, can you guess what I got for my birthday?"

"I guess a cell phone!"

"Sí! Now I can phone you any time I like. If you still want to be best friends."

"Yes! Yes! Do you?"

"Sí! Sí! Sí!"

Muchachos and *muchachas*, can you believe the two friends talked for more than an hour? They slept well that night, dreaming merry dreams. The Dream Stealer was back at his old trade and caught a witch flying on her broomstick and a zombie with rusty nails for teeth.

As far as I know, everyone lived happily ever after, except the zombie, who was troubled with toothaches.

Author's Note

I have spent a long lifetime scratching out stories. Do I ever run out of ideas? Of course. But writers keep tripping over story bones, half buried, even when they're not looking.

I was in Mexico City and, like other visitors, gawking at the art in a handicraft shop. My eye caught a hand-carved figure of some wildly imaginative and dappled creature. Who was that?

A Dream Stealer, I was told.

My writer's breath caught. A thief of dreams? What a lot of fun I could have with a character like that! I bought the sculpture, and before I left the marketplace, my mind was searching the air for plot possibilities.

When I returned home, I set the Mexican figure of the Dream Stealer on my desk for inspiration and began to write. At night I dreamed. By morning, the nightly picture shows were gone. Vanished. Stolen?

Maybe the Dream Stealer had filched them in the night.

—Sid Fleischman

Santa Monica, California

**A wily orphan, a spoiled young prince,
and an adventure neither will ever forget.**

READ ON FOR A PREVIEW OF
SID FLEISCHMAN'S NEWBERY MEDAL–WINNING
The Whipping Boy.

SID FLEISCHMAN

The Whipping Boy

JOHN NEWBERY MEDAL
FOR THE MOST DISTINGUISHED
CONTRIBUTION TO
AMERICAN LITERATURE
FOR CHILDREN

illustrations by PETER SIS

CHAPTER 1

*In which we observe
a hair-raising event*

The young prince was known here and there (and just about everywhere else) as Prince Brat. Not even black cats would cross his path.

One night the king was holding a grand feast. Sneaking around behind the lords and ladies, Prince Brat tied their powdered wigs to the backs of their oak chairs.

Then he hid behind a footman to wait.

When the guests stood up to toast the king, their wigs came flying off.

The lords clasped their bare heads as if they'd been scalped. The ladies shrieked.

Prince Brat (he was never called that to his face, of course) tried to keep from laughing. He clapped both hands over his mouth. But out it ripped, a cackle of *hah-hah*s and *haw-haw*s and *hee-hee-hee*s.

The king spied him and he looked mad enough to spit ink. He gave a furious shout.

"Fetch the whipping boy!"

Prince Brat knew that he had nothing to fear. He had never been spanked in his life. He was a prince! And it was forbidden to spank, thrash, cuff, smack, or whip a prince.

A common boy was kept in the castle to be punished in his place.

"Fetch the whipping boy!"

The king's command traveled like an echo from guard to guard up the stone stairway to a small chamber in the drafty north tower.

An orphan boy named Jemmy, the son of a rat-catcher, roused from his sleep. He'd been dreaming happily of his ragged but carefree life before he'd been plucked from the streets and sewers of the city to serve as royal whipping boy.

A guard shook him fully awake. "On your feet, me boy."

Jemmy's eyes blazed up. "Ain't I already been whipped twice today? Gaw! What's the prince done now?"

"Let's not keep the great folks waitin', lad."

In the main hall, the king said, "Twenty whacks!"

Defiantly biting back every yelp and cry, the

whipping boy received the twenty whacks. Then the king turned to the prince. "And let that be a lesson to you!"

"Yes, Papa." The prince lowered his head so as to appear humbled and contrite. But all the while he was feeling a growing exasperation with his whipping boy.

In the tower chamber, the prince fixed him with a scowl. "You're the worst whipping boy I ever had! How come you never bawl?"

"Dunno," said Jemmy with a shrug.

"A whipping boy is supposed to yowl like a stuck pig! We dress you up fancy and feed you royal, don't we? It's no fun if you don't bawl!"

Jemmy shrugged again. He was determined never to spring a tear for the prince to gloat over.

"Yelp and bellow next time. Hear? Or I'll tell

Papa to give you back your rags and kick you back into the streets."

Jemmy's spirits soared. Much obliged, Your Royal Awfulness! he thought. I'll take me rags, and I'll be gone in the half-blink of an eye.